www.trollriverpub.com
A Little Something More
The Evermore Series Book 2.5
Copyright © 2016 Rachel De Lune
ISBN: 978-1-946454-11-9

To U.S. Readers

I'd like to take this moment to let you know that Rachel is a writer living in the UK and while most terminology is the same, you may find some words or phrases odd. Knickers are underwear, "realise" is actually the correct spelling for "realize", and in the UK "flaking" is not ditching someone at a party.

Suffice it to say, if you find a word that blares out at you as "misspelled" blame the Atlantic Ocean for this diversity, not Rachel. This book has been properly edited and remains true to UK spelling and grammar. Thank you for your time!

Happy Christmas to my wonderful readers.

One

"Isabel, get down here, now! I swear you're going to be late to your own wedding," Jess barks up the stairs.

The cheval mirror reflects delicate patterns of pearls embroidered on ivory silk that traverses the curves of my body and flows effortlessly into a small train around my feet. The boning of the corseted bodice is subtle but will provide Seb a delicious treat when he gets to untie me later. The perfect dress for a perfect fairy tale day.

I inch up the hem to reveal my white lace, Louboutin wedding heels. The flash of red on the trademark sole and the delicate black and grey anklet tattooed onto my skin send a bolt of confidence to my erratic nerves. A few months ago I could never have imagined this future. Seb had turned my world around and brought me back to life. Today, I'll perform the ultimate public act of submission and marry him.

I smile to myself and take a deep breath before navigating the stairs in my four-inch heels.

"We need to leave now, Izzy! What's the hold…" Jess stops mid-yell as I glide into the front room.

"Okay. Now I'm ready, Jess."

Jess smiles, and I see warmth and pride shine in her eyes. She teeters across the carpet in her own 'death heels' and wraps me up in a hug.

The nerves I fail to keep at bay swarm into a ball of emotion that lodges in my throat threatening to break my composure. "Stop it, Jess, or I'll cry, and you'll have to do my make-up again." I sniff. "Have you got my bouquet?" I need to focus on something other than the happy tears.

"Just a minute." She ducks out of the room. "Here it is." Jess walks back in, carrying a bouquet.

"I freeze in the middle of her lounge. "Jess, you've got the wrong flowers. That isn't my bouquet."

"I know, but these are what you're having. They're from Seb."

"Seb? Why is he choosing my flowers? They aren't anything like…"

"Stop! Calm down. Read this." She passes me a hand-addressed envelope, my name written in a scrawl of dark ink. Seb's elegant, personal stationery is familiar to me. I perch on the edge of the sofa and gently peel the heavy paper open.

Dearest Isabel,

It was once tradition for the husband to pick flowers for his wife and leave them on her doorstep. These flowers are the closest I could come to that tradition, and I wanted to give you one final message.

So that we are clear, this is the meaning behind these flowers.

The red rose signifies our love. I love you with everything I am, and that will never fade.

The lily is for majesty. You hold all of the splendour I could wish for. Our story is just that—it's ours, and I am going to cherish it.

Blue hyacinths are for constancy. I am your constant. You've come so far in believing that, and I need you to hold on to that forever.

I'm not saying that everything will be smooth sailing, but we will remain constant.

The baby's breath is for everlasting love.

I'll look forward to seeing you walk towards me, ready to become my wife, holding the message I want to share with you.

I love you, Isabel York.

Always yours,

Sebastian.

The words swim in front of me as tears pool in my eyes. I grit my teeth, and my eyes tingle with the effort to stop them falling and smudging my face.

Seb has always made such romantic gestures. I haven't always understood them, but he's certainly topped them all with this. He's so much more than I ever could have dreamed of. The friendship that had first blossomed between us had grown immeasurably. I'd always trusted Seb, but somehow that trust had strengthened with time. His care as my Dom and as my partner allowed me to grow in confidence and express myself. I was finally the woman that had been imprisoned within my insecurities. I was Seb's partner—yes, I submitted to him, but I knew that he cherished that submission and the D/s element of our lives enriched the rest of our time together. He let me grow and didn't want to hold me back. It was part of the reason why I finally agreed to marry him. With his gentle guidance and constant support, he let me find my own path. I felt like a new Izzy. One that could hold her head up and didn't have to lock her fantasies away on the computer. With Seb, I live them every day.

I pick up the flowers and can't help but love every single bloom. He's banished the nerves and given me something to hold onto as I walk down the aisle.

3

Jess hovers beside me, exuding impatience. As she's already pointed out, we'd better get moving. There was no way I wanted to be late for Seb.

Jess' Dad drives us to the hotel in Seb's Audi A5. I wanted him to be part of my day. He's been a surrogate father figure to me as I've seen far more of Jess' parents than my own over the years.

We're quiet on the short drive into Bath. The Royal Crescent Hotel is our destination, and the weather couldn't be better. A crisp, winter's day greets us. The sunshine lights up the day and banishes the usual grey. The bare branches of an oak tree are silhouetted against a bright blue sky as we drive up towards the Crescent.

I feel a shiver of excitement as we approach our final destination. The building's soft sandstone gleams in the winter sun. Jess leans forward and takes my hand in support as the car slows down and pulls up outside the pillared entrance. I take a deep breath and clutch at the flowers resting in my lap.

The name of the hotel was certainly appropriate. The stately venue was stunning, from the liveried doorman to the luxurious textured fabrics that swathed the windows and softened each grand room within. I even felt regal when Seb and I came to visit. Nothing was too much trouble, and I felt like the most important woman in the world. Of course, most of that was due to Seb.

The Georgian building was awe-worthy, and the suite that Seb and I would share tonight was the pinnacle of opulence. It held enough space to host a small party, although I know Seb had something more private in mind. The antique four-poster bed with its silk and velvet bed linens looked small in the spacious room. Down-cushioned armchairs and loveseats were arranged in front of the working fireplace. Hues of pale, egg-shell blue complimented lush olive green across the walls and furnishings. The marble bathroom was like stepping into your personal spa and came fully stocked with lotions and creams from Aromatherapy Associates. The small dressing table held an antique hand mirror and brush set, with a cut glass scent bottle to the side. Not a single detail was out of place.

At first, I didn't want to get married at such a desirable address. But I fell in love with the romance of the place. Hundreds of years of visitors and guests through the doors. I found it hard not to get swept up in the thrill. The hotel would be a perfect backdrop to our day.

I see Natasha standing outside the front of the hotel. She's her usual stunning self. Her burgundy lace dress fits her like a glove. I can't help but smile as I think how intimidating she can be. Now, all I see is a strong, beautiful woman. *Until we enter Solace.*

Natasha opens the car door once we're stationary and Jess offers me her hand to help me out of the car. She fluffs my train to ensure it's neatly flared before I take Mr. Riley's arm. He escorts me through the entrance where I see my parents. My Dad looks extremely handsome in his tailored suit, and Mum smiles warmly as she catches my eye.

"We'll see you in there, Izzy. You look wonderful." Mr. Riley gives me a brief squeeze before handing me over to my Dad.

"All okay?" he asks.

"Yes, Dad. A few nerves perhaps."

"Oh, that's only natural, dear. You look radiant." Mum leans in to air kiss my cheek. "I'll see you in there." She squeezes my hand and heads into the library where the ceremony will take place.

My limbs begin to buzz with a shaky nervousness. I take a few steps around, fidgeting with my dress, my flowers, anything to distract myself.

"Izzy, relax. Now." Natasha's firm words cut through the butterflies and centre me.

I can do this. I want to do this.

"Get out of your head, Izzy and think about Seb. You good?"

I stare at her beautiful, composed face and wish I could be calm.

"Yes. Thank you, Natasha."

"No problem." She turns away and lingers by the double doors that lead our way into the library. Jess joins her, waiting for me to signal that I'm ready.

Today might not be the first time I've stood waiting to walk down the aisle to the man I love, but I knew, in the very heart of my soul, that this time would be different. Seb was my missing piece. He completes me, and I'm able to complete him. He made me happy and set me free.

All the reasons why I'm standing here fill my heart with sheer joy. I nod to Jess, take Dad's arm and stand behind Jess and Natasha.

The door to the ceremony room opens, and I hear the rustle of bodies twisting in their chairs to watch as I walk towards Seb. The piano begins the first few notes of Christina Perri's, _A Thousand Years_ and we wait for the strings to join in the melody. Jess and Natasha take a few steps forward and move gracefully down the chair-lined aisle.

I take a breath and straighten. I smile at my Dad and then lock my focus on my man.

Seb steps into view at the front of the room and sets my heart racing. Those pesky tears are burning my eyes, and I force myself not to give in. I want Seb to see me happy, not tear-stained.

My cheeks quiver as I try and hold my smile, fighting with the emotion that is now pulsating around my body. Dad takes controlled steps forward, keeping pace with the music and I let him lead. Seb is devastating in his tailored suit. The fabric sculpts his broad shoulders and reminds me of what's under the shirt.

My steps bring me closer and closer to Seb, and I see his handsome face taut with the same emotion that I'm fighting inside.

Jess peels off to sit to one side while Natasha takes her place next to Seb. Dad comes to a stop, and Seb nods towards my Dad and then his gaze rests on me.

"Hi," I whisper.

"Hi," Seb replies.

"Thank you for the flowers. They are perfect."

"Couldn't resist one last message to you." He takes my hand, and we turn towards the registrar.

The ceremony proceeds with a welcome address. Seb maintains a firm grip on my hand, and I use his strength to conquer my overwhelming emotions. I may have opposed getting married again, but right now, I know I want to be Seb's wife just as much as he wants to be my husband.

_8_

The registrar continues with the formalities before turning to Seb.

"Sebastian, you have a few words." Seb faces me. He takes the flowers from my grasp and hands them to Jess.

"Izzy. I love you with everything I am, and that will never fade. You hold all the splendour I could wish for, and I promise to cherish you and our love. I am your constant, and I'll guide you to wherever you want to go in life. You hold my vows in your hands, and I am proud to stand before our family and friends and share my love for you. I promise compassion and love in everything we do."

My heart bursts with the love I have for this man. Every atom of my being begs to echo his words back to him. I resist throwing my arms around his neck and pulling him to me as closely as I can.

"Sebastian, will you repeat after me... I do solemnly declare that I know not of any lawful impediment why I, Sebastian York may not be joined in matrimony to Isabel Fields."

I stare, transfixed at Seb's lips as he speaks the words that will bind us as man and wife.

I follow the registrar's words and make my declaration. The registrar again turns to Seb. "Will you, Seb, take Izzy to be your wedded wife, to share your life, to love her and support her, whatever the future may hold?"

"I will." The deep timbre of Seb's reply pulls at my heart, and another wave of euphoria crashes over me.

"Will you, Izzy, take Seb to be your wedded husband, to share your life, to love him and support him, whatever the future may hold?"

"I will." I push the words past the lump in my throat and feel the tension ease from my body at my decree. I look into Seb's aqua eyes and feel our connection hum through my body.

9

My words are more to him than just agreeing to be his wife. I'm giving him my submission.

"Izzy, I give you this ring as a sign of our marriage. May it always remind you of our unwavering love and commitment. A symbol of our love and our forever more." Seb slides the platinum band dotted with tiny diamonds along my finger and brushes over it with his thumb.

I take Seb's ring from Natasha and mirror the words he just spoke to me. My voice catches as the power of this moment hits me in my chest.

Seb is my husband.

Three

Jess and Natasha follow us from the library into the garden room as man and wife.

Seb has a death-grip on my hand but a wicked smile on his lips. I suddenly don't want to be social and celebrate with friends. I want to be alone with my husband.

A waiter approaches and presents a silver platter with bubbling glasses of champagne. Seb takes a glass and hands me a flute.

"Cheers, Mrs. York."

"Cheers, Mr. York." The chime of our glasses is drowned out as our guests flood into the room behind us. Our friends and family engulf us with congratulations. I can't shift the smile from my face, and I don't want to. I can't remember a happier time.

For the next two hours, my feet are hardly still. They only rest for the quick snap of a photo before being manoeuvred into another position. I'm sure that I'll look back fondly on all of the images and be glad that I can re-live this day with such a detailed photographic account. But right now, I want to sit down with my husband.

"Are we nearly done?"

"We can be done as soon as you say the word."

"I'm done. I don't need any more pictures." Seb's smile lights me up, and I watch as he turns towards the photographer and takes him to the side.

"What's Seb doing, Iz?" Jess asks.

"Moving things along I believe. I'm done with the photos."

"Oh thank god. I need to be out of these heels. Why did you have to make me wear them again?" Jess huffs and bends down to remove her shoes. "Arr, that's better. If we're done, I'm not putting these back on."

"Okay, hun. Thank you for tolerating them today."

"Only for you, Izzy. Only for you." She leans in and gives me a quick kiss before heading off on her own.

Seb crosses the room towards me, and I feel his eyes trail over my body. His look alone can heat my blood and send my pulse into orbit. Now that the important part is complete, my mind strays to what Seb has in store for this evening.

Seb's fingers caress my bare arms and send a ripple of goosebumps over my body.

"It won't be much longer until I can have you all to myself, Mrs. York. Don't think for one moment that I won't savour every second we're alone tonight." His whispered promise resonates as if he shouted the words at me. His fingers find my hands and he leads me into the banquet room across from the quaint room we've been using.

Half a dozen round tables are decked out in pristine linen table cloths. Cream covers encase the chairs, and all of the neutral tones are set off against elegant displays of stargazer lilies in the centre vases. It's everything I could have wished for. The room oozes warmth with its neutral shades and low light, the romance of the day follows us. I squeeze Seb's hand a little harder. As we make our way to our table and he seats me, I catch sight of a flustered hotel employee heading out the other door. I guess Seb moved up the schedule.

"Ladies and gentleman, may I have your attention." Seb's commanding voice leaves our guests no room to disobey.

"Thank you. We are breaking with tradition when it comes to the speeches. Natasha, as my best woman won't be causing me any embarrassment. Thank you, Natasha." I tilt back in my chair to catch the smug look she wears. "But I would still like to say a few words. You've already heard me make my vows to Izzy, and I can say that nothing in the world will make me happier than she has done today by marrying me. She is the woman I've been waiting to come into my life, and now I have her..." he turns to me before finishing his sentence..."I won't be letting you go." A vice-like grip squeezes my heart at his words. The communal murmur that follows tells me it's not just me feeling the meaning behind them.

"We'd both like to thank our closest friends and family for being here as witnesses today and for all of the support you've given to us over the past months. Please raise your glasses to friends and family." I look to Jess as I raise my glass. She has been my rock, and I wouldn't be here today without her. She downs the remaining champagne in her glass before looking for the next one.

The rest of the evening is a test of both our patience.

Stolen glances, sweet kisses and an all too brief dance in Seb's arms, keep the underlying sexual tension simmering between us.

The party is in full swing, and our friends fill the dance floor. A party isn't where I want to be. I go in search of Seb, ready for him to take me upstairs. He's standing at the bar with

Natasha. I lean against the doorframe and wait for him to spot me. I know it won't be long—it's as if he can sense me when I'm close.

Sure enough, he pauses in his conversation and looks towards me. A grin tugs at the corner of his lips. An unspoken communication passes between us at that moment. His posture hardens, and I watch as he excuses himself. He prowls across the floor. That invisible switch has been flicked, the one that sets desire loose in my body.

"If you tell me you want to stay down here, I'll understand. But I can't fucking wait to get you to myself." The scrape of his stubble grates against my neck as he nips at my ear.

"Do we have to say good night to everyone?" I tease.

"No fucking way. We've been polite, celebrated, and enjoyed the day. Now it's my turn to enjoy my wife."

He plants a demanding kiss on my lips, sending my pulse skyrocketing. The lacing on my dress halts my attempt to take a deep breath. All I want now is for Seb to strip it off me. His lips slow and give me time to catch my breath. He takes my hand and pulls me behind him in his haste to exit our party.

Four

We make it unhindered to the stairs and up to our suite. Anticipation flares inside me and sends a bolt of lust through my veins. Seb opens our room and makes a purposeful show of slamming the door and locking it behind us.

"No interruptions. Just you and me."

I stand frozen in place in the middle of the room waiting for Seb's instruction. His gaze assesses every nuance of my body as I wait. The longer his eyes stay on me, the hotter I become. My lips part as my breathing falters.

"Stay where you are. Let me take my fill of you." Seb prowls around me, keeping out of arm's reach. I've learned to relax under his gaze and to have confidence that he enjoys looking at me. He's certainly spent a long time staring at me over the last few months. Mostly when I'm naked or in varying states of undress.

"You're exquisite. You've always been beautiful to me, but today you are radiant. I love seeing you happy. But I think I've seen enough of the dress, baby." He steps closer to me, and it takes all of my willpower not to wrap my arms around him and pull his lips to mine. I know not to rush Seb and wait for his instruction. "Turn around and hold onto the corner post of our bed. Use it to support yourself."

I grasp the post and continue to wait. I resist the urge to fidget. With this dress on, any movement is amplified. It doesn't stop me from wanting to press my thighs together in an attempt to suppress the growing ache.

The deep pile carpet silences Seb's movements, and with my back to him, I'm left to my imagination. My ears strain to hear movement, and I'm rewarded with a muted thud that I hope is his jacket.

"So perfect, waiting for my command."

Feather light touches trace patterns up my side, avoiding the wide laced-up back of the dress. I slide my eyes closed and picture the flow of his touch. Curves and spirals dance through my mind. He's tracing the patterns of embroidery and pearls sewn onto my dress.

His fingers grow bolder as I feel the gentle tug on the silk ribbons that hold my dress together. My grip on the post tightens as he loosens the ties, jolting my body with each pull.

"You've given me the greatest submission by agreeing to be my wife. But I want more," he growls out the final words, turning them from romantic to sexy. "Spread your legs a bit wider."

I step wider, careful not to get my heel stuck in the carpet and lean harder against the bed post.

Seb continues working me out of my dress. I feel some of the pressure release from around my chest, but I have a bonus for him tonight. His hands cage my ribs, and he slides the dress from my body revealing another layer of lace as he does. The gown pools at my feet, but he'll be able to see the outfit I chose just for him.

"Jesus, woman. You're killing me, and I've barely touched you."

I smile, knowing what he's looking at. A white lace panelled corset cinches my waist and supports my breasts. I've forgone knickers as I knew Seb would approve. The finest, sheer hold-ups cover my legs and lead down to my favourite heels, although they are hidden by my dress until I can move.

My breaths quicken with the expectation of his touch, and my pussy is aching for attention. Again I wait. I lock my arms and hold myself with the confidence that Seb has fostered within me. I open my eyes and move my hand so I can look at the rings on my finger. They twinkle in the soft light of the room.

"You look fucking delicious, Izzy, and I'm having a hard time being patient. I wanted tonight to be about us. No playing games, no rules. But I think we can get to that. Step out of your dress and let me see you properly."

I stand up and step free of the dress and the bed. Seb is sitting in one of the armchairs, shirt sleeves exposing his forearms, top button undone, looking more handsome than ever. Now he really *is* mine.

"Come here. If I try and remove that corset, I'll end up shredding it. You can do it for me." He points to a spot in front of him. I walk to it and pull myself up, feeding off the knowledge that this man means the world to me.

It's my turn to tease, and I delicately unhook the first of the many tiny eyelets strapping me in. One by one they free my breasts, and they spill from their confinement. I work lower and lower until I can toss the lace to the side.

I can finally take a deep breath, and I fill my lungs with much-needed oxygen.

"If I touch you, will you be wet for me?"

I smile, enjoying hearing the deep tones of Seb's Dom voice.

"Yes, Sir."

"Did I tell you not to wear knickers today?"

"No, Sir."

"And you failed to mention that fact until now?"

"I thought it could be a nice surprise for you." I try and keep some of the sass out of my voice and fail. I hear the clink of his belt and watch as he frees his cock from his trousers, stroking it from root to head.

He reaches and trails his free hand down the outside of my thigh. Every nerve fibre tingles with recognition, and I suppress the moan that threatens to creep past my lips. His fingers work their way to the apex of my thighs, and he runs a single finger through my pussy. This time, the moan escapes and my head falls back in pleasure. I've been waiting all day to feel his intimate caress.

"I want you to straddle me, fuck me until you come. Then we'll get back to me worshipping you as my wife." Seb shoves his trousers down further and kicks off his shoes.

We've barely kissed today, and the need to be close to Seb palpitates through my body. With my heels and hold-ups still on, I kneel over his lap and rest my hands on his toned shoulders.

I dip my head and let our lips brush. Seb inhales audibly and wraps his arms around my waist. My lips work harder, sucking and teasing until they beg for his surrender. He finally gives into the kiss and allows me to deepen it as I lower my body.

I press my slick heat against his rigid cock and grind down. The friction sparks a torrent of arousal through my body that breaks the fragile control I thought I had.

Our tongues duel and the air saturates with the breathy moans and pants from both of us. I tip my hips back and forth working my sensitive flesh with every thrust. His fingers dig into my hips as he anchors me in position. He breaks our kiss and begins a hurried exploration of my neck and chest until he reaches my breasts. He licks around my nipple before sucking it into his warm mouth.

"Arrr!" I moan. The deep ache within me builds as Seb flicks at my nipples.

"I thought I told you to fuck me."

"Yes… god, yes."

I lift above him to give myself room, and he positions the head of his thick shaft at my entrance. I slowly sink, enveloping him in my heat. I pause, giving myself a moment to adjust before rocking against him. I arch and thrust, driving him as deep as I can take him. As I surge forward, I grind my clit against the bottom of his shaft and my body tightens in anticipation of the orgasm I'm holding at bay. My muscles tense and heat flushes my exposed skin.

Seb sits back, and I struggle to keep my eyes open and on him.

"You're close, baby." He drives his hips up, hitting that spot that makes me lose all coherent thought. He repeats and my orgasm thunders through me. My lust-fuelled cries echo in the room as my heartbeat drums in my ears.

At some point, my eyes slide shut, and I collapse forward against Seb's chest.

"You're still pulsing around my dick."

I don't answer. My body screams for air, and I take deep pulls to fill my lungs. I can feel that Seb didn't come. A pang of disappointment pulses in my chest, but he doesn't let me dwell for long. He lifts me and carries my spent body back to the grand bed.

He rests me on the bed, and I watch through half-shut eyes as he admires my naked body.

"You're all mine, sweetheart—every delectable inch of you—and I'm going to enjoy you how I'd planned." He pulls my ankle towards him and slips my four-inch stiletto from my foot. The creep of his hands up my legs sends a riot of sensation straight to my core. He slips his fingers under the elastic of the hold-ups and slides them free. He repeats his torturously sexy routine on my other leg. My body, tired and spent from a few moments ago, awakes under his touch.

He cradles my tattooed ankle in his hand and begins to trace the black and grey lines of ink. His touch both soothes and titillates. Just before I start to relax, his lips follow the same path. Soft caresses and nips start at my ankle before travelling higher.

By the time he reaches the delicate spot behind my knee, I want to beg him to hurry up. My body trembles with anticipation, and I have no idea how I'm going to survive much more of his focused and meticulous attention.

"Please, Seb. I want you." My plea is full of the lust I feel towards my husband.

"I want to take my time and show you how much today means to me." His teeth dig into my inner thigh, emphasising his words. The bite sends a bolt of need to my pussy, and I squirm into the duvet.

Seb drops my leg and climbs onto the bed. He settles himself between my thighs and resumes his slow worship of my body.

His lips traverse across the planes of my body until he sucks the tight bud of my nipple into his mouth. I arch in delight as strikes of longing resonate in my sex. Primed for his touch, my body cries out for something harder, something more fulfilling from him.

"Please, Seb…"

"Shh. Enjoy my touch, or I'll tie you up." His teeth bite down in warning, but it's not one that I'll heed. His pain is as much of a turn on as his pleasure.

I clench my jaw tight and let the sensations wash over me as Seb continues. Touch, kiss, caress, lick… he doesn't stop until every inch of my skin has felt him. My breath labours and my sex slicks with desire.

"I want you to remember how you feel. I want you to know how much I care for you; how much I love you." Seb teases my lips between words, his gravely voice betraying his restraint.

His body presses into mine and heat flares through me as our bodies finally connect skin to skin. Desperation claws in my chest as I hope Seb will finally give me the relief I crave.

He positions his cock and slides easily into me. My sigh of release reverberates through my chest. Seb holds himself deep within me before pulling out and thrusting back in. His rotation skims my swollen clit, and my arousal surges higher.

"God… you feel fucking amazing. I want you to come again, baby."

"Yes, Seb… please. Harder!"

I'd had enough of the soft and tender. Luckily, Seb agreed and powered into me, forcing a moan from my throat.

"Yes… Seb… Yes!" My limbs go weak as my climax rips through my body. I pulse in time with my racing heart as the waves of release wash over me.

"Oh, fuck!" Seb cries before burying his head in the crook of my neck. I feel his teeth bite on my shoulder but don't register more than the warmth of his lips.

He collapses on me, both our bodies spent and slippery with sweat.

"God, I love you."

"I love you, too."

Five

Six weeks have passed in the blink of an eye.

Seb flew me to New York for an incredible honeymoon. He redefined the term 'wined and dined'. Everything was perfect—a lovely balance of private time spent locked away in our extravagant hotel room, seeing the sites of New York and visiting with his parents. His mother is the most gracious, kind woman I think I've ever met. I wanted to bring her home with us. I hope she'll come and stay in the future.

I had planned on having an easy few weeks after our return, but it was my time to step up and be there for Jess. After all the tragedy in her past, she needed something to go her way in the love department. My fear was that she'd be too stubborn to see it.

"When do you want to put up the tree?" I call out, looking at our sparse living room.

"I don't have a tree. I don't usually bother with Christmas," Seb responds.

My eyes widen in disbelief. I head into the kitchen to question my new husband.

"Do you have decorations? Christmas paraphernalia that we can decorate the house with?"

"No."

"Nothing?" I'm astonished.

"No. I've never really had the need to celebrate Christmas as you do. I've been in New York visiting my parents or working. Collecting 'stuff' to put away in storage for eleven months of the year hasn't been a priority."

Seb's reasoning is sound, but I still struggle to understand it. For me, Christmas is a wonderful time of year. The air fills with a unique magic and never fails to lift my spirits. The last few years were the exception, and now that those times are past, I am as excited as a child waiting for Father Christmas.

I want to create memories Seb and I will cherish. I want to build a life full of traditions and celebrations. We reconnected and got to spend our first Christmas together just a year ago. That was a start, but I want more.

It is the beginning of December, which means the Bath Christmas Market will still be on for a few weeks. My body fills with excitement as I picture us walking through the bustling streets of Bath, soaking up the atmosphere.

"Have you ever been to the Christmas Market?" I ask, anticipation ringing in my voice.

"No, but I take it from the look on your face that we'll be going."

I throw my arms around his neck. "Yes, yes we will," and kiss his luscious lips.

Three days later, my excitement has reached its height. Much like our short trip around Manchester last year, I let Seb bundle me up before we take a walk over to the abbey and market.

We stroll, hand in hand, under the night glow of the city towards the centre of Bath. The frigid wind sends my hair whipping around my face, but I don't care. The rich aroma of spices, oranges and wine infuse the air as we turn into the main market area. Chalet huts, glittering with fairy lights, line the square and emit an enticing glow of warm light. Christmas revellers pack the pavements, bustling about, and I bask in the magic that the scene creates.

"Where do you want to start?" Seb asks, pulling me from my daze.

"Over there." I point to a hut with glistening balls of iridescent glass hanging from rainbow ribbons. The ornaments look beautiful, and I immediately picture a tall tree with the small globes adorning the branches.

I 'ooh' and 'aah' over the handmade decorations and turn to Seb.

"Don't look to me. You choose. We're starting this from scratch so whatever you want is fine." He leans forward and places his lips to my forehead.

I find a clerk. "I'll have six gold and six random colours, please."

We spend the next hour weaving in and out of the rows of stalls, buying decorations and gifts for our first Christmas. Dazzling paper star lights, glass Christmas trees, fabric angles and ornamental snow globes are all carefully wrapped inside the bags we carry.

"Fancy some mulled wine or mulled cider?"

"That sounds great."

Seb heads towards one of the chalets with vats of Christmas cheer steaming away. We take our cups and find a seat in front of the giant spruce tree that forms the centrepiece. The only thing missing from this scene is a flurry of snow.

"What are you thinking? You look whimsical."

"I'm just thinking how perfect this is. And that the only thing missing is snow."

Seb chuckles and I can't help the bubble of giggles that escapes. "You know there's often snow in New York City at this time of year. Perhaps next year, we could spend Christmas with my parents."

"Sounds like a plan. I like your Mum."

"And she adores you. Are you happy sitting here or do you want to do more shopping?"

We'd only gone around half of the market, but I was near exhausted. All this furore had taken it out of me. I wanted to finish the evening snuggled up in Seb's arms.

"I'm pretty tired. Can we head home? We have the weekend to get the house looking festive."

"Of course."

We finish the warming drinks and meander back towards home.

I leave the bags of goodies on the kitchen table and head into the front room to collapse. I was exhausted, and the mulled wine didn't help with my sleepiness. I hear Seb's footsteps as he comes in to join me. "Did you enjoy the market?" I ask, my eyes already closed.

"Yes. You were in your element, and I loved watching your excitement bubble over. Will this be a family tradition then?"

"Definitely, although I think we can cut back on the decorations next year." I pull my feet up under me and snuggle down on the sofa.

"Hey, if you're that tired we can go up to bed."

"But I want to sleep."

"Who said I couldn't take you to bed and let you sleep?" I don't have to open my eyes to see his wide grin. His mirth is clear from his words.

My body fights with my mind as I try and come around from my deep slumber. Heavy eyelids hinder my progress. I stretch and turn to Seb, only to find his half of the bed empty and cold. The fog of sleep clears as I search for the time. It's nearly 11:00 a.m. I haven't slept this long in forever. I pull back the duvet and grab my robe before going in search of Seb.

The smell of coffee wafts up the stairs as I head down to meet it. I peek inside the front room and find Seb. Tears sting the back of my eyes, and my throat swells with emotion as I watch him. Delight hums through every fibre of my body. He stands in front of a seven-foot tree, adorning the branches with a few of the ornaments we brought yesterday.

"I hope you don't mind. I started without you. You were out of it, and I wanted to let you sleep." I pad into the room and wrap my arms around his waist to squeeze him tightly. This man is my everything. It's not just the grandiose gestures, but the small things, like helping with the tree, which have created such a powerful connection between us.

"Thank you. When did you get the tree?"

"This morning. I wanted us to be able to spend the day doing Christmas stuff. Like you wanted."

"It's perfect. Or at least it will be once we've finished. I love you."

"I love you."

The tree's boughs are still sparsely decorated, and I can't wait to dig into the bags and unwrap the ornaments.

We spend the next hour wrapping twinkle lights around the branches and hanging baubles and angels on our tree. We don't talk but share smiles as we finish our first Christmas tree.

"Is it bad that I want to have this Christmas all to ourselves?" My question comes out as a whine as we cuddle on the sofa admiring our handy work.

"No, it's not bad. Remember, we had last Christmas all to ourselves. We have plenty of time before your Mum and Dad arrive to have our own time together, and your parents will only be with us for a few days."

"I know. I'm being selfish. I'm just… I'm happy. I'm filled with happiness, and I'm not sure I want anything to burst this bubble."

"Hey," Seb pulls me closer into him, "nothing is going to burst our bubble. This is our life now."

"Are you happy here? We still haven't found a house to buy."

"I'm happy here with you as long as you are."

The tears that threatened earlier return, but this time win and trickle down my cheek. I hold my breath to try and keep them from falling and dash away the salty evidence on my face before Seb notices. "Do you want a drink? I'll put the kettle on." I escape out of the room and take a deep breath as I head to the kitchen. The urge to cry abates as I focus on the remedial task of making a cup of tea.

* * *

After the charm and joy of decorating the tree, the normality of life seeps back in. Seb is at work and a mountain of client projects to review hide my desk in my office. We're both still catching up from our honeymoon, and since Christmas is just around the corner, the daydreams of creating more 'first' memories slip further away.

I leave work and get home before Seb. The warm glow of the lights from the tree greet me as I enter the dark house. Despite our busy work schedule, I can still feel Christmas in the air. I set about preparing dinner, unsure of when Seb will be home.

I open and close every cupboard in the kitchen trying to find inspiration for what to cook. Nothing takes my fancy, so I opt for my fall back. I set a pan of water on the stove, grab a red pepper from the fridge and start to chop. I prepare the garlic and pepper and dose with a generous helping of olive oil and leave it in the pan for when Seb walks in.

> I've got dinner covered. When will you be home?
> xx

I wait for his answering text and curl up on the sofa in the front room.

The door slamming closed startles me, and I bolt up from the sofa.

"Iz, I'm sorry. I got held up at work. Did you eat already?" Seb calls from the hall, and I blink my eyes a few times to orientate myself. Seb walks in and joins me. "Hey, were you asleep?"

"Yeah, sorry. I just closed my eyes for a moment. What time is it?"

"Nearly half eight. Did you eat?"

"No, no. I got it all ready. We just need to get the pasta on."

"Are you okay?" Seb curls a loose strand of hair around my ear and tilts my head up to look at him.

"I'm fine. Come on. Let's get us fed." Seb takes my hand and pulls me up. I don't miss the quizzical look he gives me as I pass him.

Fifteen minutes later, we're sitting at the table with a bowl of pasta and a glass of wine.

"I know it's not long until your parents will be here. I've been thinking of a way to celebrate before they arrive. We've not been to Solace on our own since before our honeymoon. I think it's time we made some room for it." Seb grins across the table at me.

"I think that would be a wonderful idea, Sir."

"Good girl. Next Friday night. I want you home on time. I'll have chosen the clothes I want you to wear, and I'll leave them in the spare room. We'll eat, celebrate before we enjoy the rest of the evening together." My mind goes into overdrive as I imagine the possibilities, and I have my Christmas treat to look forward to.

"I'm looking forward to it already."

"Oh, and one more thing. You're not allowed to come until next Friday. I want you pent-up and frustrated for what I have in store." My stomach drops at his command. My eyes lower from his face, and I force my body to stay still, although I'm desperate to fidget. I rub my wedding bands with my thumb. It was a habit I had, and although I don't want to associate anything of my old life with the new one I share with Seb, I simply can't help myself.

My body still responds so vividly to Seb. We've grown accustomed to living together, waking up and going about our day. The every day hasn't diluted the connection that first pulled us together.

"Now, as beautiful as you look there, I want to enjoy you in our bedroom. Go upstairs, strip, and wait for me on the bed. Do not touch yourself, understand."

"Yes, Sir."

Seven

This week has been the longest in forever. Or should I say, the longest since Seb had previously forbidden me to come. We were apart then. With us sleeping in the same bed every night, it brought a new level of exasperation to my world. I grew more amorous each night as Seb played my body like a master with passionate kisses that made me feel drunk and tender touches that had me begging for him to be aggressive. Seb ensured that I was at my wits' end by the middle of the week. The climax-freeze wasn't a mutually agreed term. He enjoyed me sucking the silky head of his cock to the back of my throat while I was positioned ready for his tongue to torture me. My problem was he enjoyed my pussy aching with need. He withheld any touch that I craved. His fingers didn't even skim the swollen and tender flesh between my thighs. He tormented me with his body and lips and left me with a burning knot of frustration in the pit of my stomach.

Friday morning finally arrived. My alarm woke me first, and I start our day as I have done so many others. I make the coffee, deliver it back to our room, and kiss Seb awake. The nerves I used to feel at what could come from my submission have morphed into butterflies of excitement. I no longer fear what might occur when I put myself in Seb's hands. He's proved time and time again why I trust him and has shown me the rewards of that trust.

His lips gently press back against mine, and he deepens the kiss. Today, Seb is in control. My eager and strung out body responds in kind and I move my leg to straddle Seb's body. I grind down to try and generate some much-needed friction.

"Stop. I told you I wanted you frustrated for tonight. I want you to melt into my touch. Understand."

"Yes, Sir."

He hoists me off of him and heads for the shower. I snuggle back in bed and sip my coffee until he's finished.

"I've put the clothes for work and then this evening in the spare room. I'll be checking in with you through the day. Have you got anything on at work that I need to be aware of?"

"No, my diary's pretty clear today, Sir. When will you be home?"

"By six at the latest. I want you ready when I walk through the door, understand."

"Yes."

"Yes, what?"

"Sorry, yes, Sir."

"I bet you'll be wet for me before I even get home."

I squeeze my eyes shut and try and think of something other than the sexy timbre of his voice and how it's precisely tuned to have the maximum effect on me.

"You'll be so slick you better be careful at work. None of those suggestions I used to fill your mind with."

I bury myself under the covers in a lame attempt to escape him.

"Don't worry. I'll have you screaming soon enough." He snaps the sheets back, divesting me of my temporary hiding place. He dresses and then offers a chase kiss in parting before heading out the door.

Once I hear the front door close, I venture into the spare room to see what I'll be wearing today and this evening. Two outfits are displayed against the wardrobe door. I can't miss them, but when I see my evening's attire, I wish I had.

A sheer lace robe drapes from the arms of the hanger. A wide edge of black silk is the only solid part of the outfit. Filigree and patterns adorn the full length of the gown but offer no concealment. My heart beats loudly in my chest at his challenge. This is by far the most revealing of anything he's laid out for me in the past.

I slide it from the hanger and hope that there is some hidden underwear. There is none. The silk edging will run down the centre of my body and offer a margin of concealment. My nipples, breasts and whole body will be visible to anyone and everyone at Solace. Waiting for my attention on the floor are a matching pair of black and lace heels. They soften the blow of the shocking negligee, and I sit back on the bed before casting my eyes to my more pressing challenge.

I don't even bother to scan the hanging garments I'll be wearing at work for underwear. I know there won't be any. He's picked my high waisted pencil skirt and teamed it with a white blouse. This would normally be the kind of outfit I'd pick for myself. But the shirt has a deep vee, and with no bra, it's certainly risque.

Seb hasn't challenged me in this way since before the wedding, and I'm flung back to all the times in the past where I've struggled to balance my need to please him with what I'm confident doing. I twirl my anklet or the tattoo that represents my anklet, and my thumb rubs over my rings.

I am not the same insecure girl that constantly questioned and analysed everything. I don't need to muster my courage. I have the confidence to pull this off because I know Seb would never ask too much of me. Plus, I long to feel the rush of hearing Seb's praise.

Half an hour later, I'm wearing the sexy outfit and even take a quick selfie to send to Seb.

> Enjoy your morning. Love Izzy x
>
> You've certainly given me something to enjoy. S x

Seb's texts punctuate a day that is otherwise uneventful. There are no raised eyebrows or comments about my choice of clothes and no situations that made me feel too uncomfortable.

All day, all I want is to get home to wait for Seb. Lust simmers under each exchange and has me checking the clock every half an hour.

Finally, 5:00 p.m.and I'm out of the office without a backwards glance and home by 5:30 p.m. The floor is the resting place for the skirt and blouse as I rush for a quick shower.

I feel like an excitable child finally getting the present she'd always asked for. Energy pumped through my veins and a smile lights up my face as I get ready for our date. I pile my hair into a messy bun and tease a few locks to frame my face.

The fabric of the robe glides over my skin as I put it on. I position the centre panel to offer myself as much modesty as I can but enjoy the overall look in the mirror. Seb told me I'd be wet by the time he got home, and he won't be wrong. I ease into the beautiful heels and take in the finished look before sitting in the small chair in the room.

The minutes creep past, and I have to try some calming breaths to relax. I shouldn't be this excited about going to Solace with Seb. We've done it dozens of times in the past. There's something in the air that makes tonight special. Maybe being so close to Christmas, and that we're giving each other this time together. The expectancy gets the better of me, and I stand to go and find my phone.

I'll be leaving in 10. Be ready. S

It was the last message from Seb, and he sent it over half an hour ago. He should be home any minute. I attempt patience and perch on the edge of the bed. I cross my legs and my dress for the evening parts, revealing my naked legs underneath. It certainly has the show stopping factor to it.

"Shit!" I'd completely forgotten that I should be downstairs with wine waiting for him. I hustle from the bedroom in my adorable new heels and pull the wine from the fridge. I pour two glasses and take a sip, giving my pulse time to recover. I take a seat at the kitchen table and listen for the door.

The minutes stretch out, and I grow increasingly impatient. I've sipped all I dare of my wine.

Everything ok? Izzy x

Forty-five minutes late didn't usually warrant a check in, but Seb was never late when we had plans. The passion that had been in abundance all day was markedly absent.

I'm sorry. Still at work. I won't be much longer. S

I mentally curse his job and take my wine into the front room to wait. All of my excitement had evaporated at his text. He might still make it home in the next hour, but it doesn't stop the disappointment that worms its way through me.

I tuck my feet underneath me and pull the blanket from the back of the sofa.

Keep me posted. Missing you. X

I empty the small glass of wine over the next half hour as I try and distract myself on social media. It doesn't work.

I'm so sorry. I've got to be here for a little longer. I'll make it up to you. I love you S

My vision blurs as I read the words. I shouldn't be upset. Seb stays late and works long hours a lot of the time. I knew that from the start. But this was the first time he hadn't made it home when he said he would.

"Izzy. Izzy, wake up." Seb shakes me, and I rock gently as I come around from my sleep.

"Seb? What time is it?" Sleep clogs my throat making my voice husky and low.

"Just after nine. I'm sorry I'm so late. We had a last minute crisis that I needed to speak to the lawyers about. I promise I'll make it up to you." His smile doesn't meet his eyes, and I can see he's sorry for letting me down.

"That's fine. I know you would have been here if you could." I stifle a yawn as I sit up. Seb offers me his hand, and I take it.

"I have to say you look delicious and can I say again how sorry I am that we haven't had our evening." He pulls me into him, and I wrap my arms around his neck. I'm pleased he's home, but I'm finding it hard to get excited again.

He must sense my mood because he pulls me tighter before whispering, "Do you want to go up to bed?"

"Yes, if you don't mind. I know we had all sorts of plans for tonight, but right now I'm struggling to keep my eyes open. Even wearing this gown." A shy smile pulls at the corner of my lips, and Seb tucks me under his arm.

"I've had a hellish evening myself. Bed, with you, sounds like the best plan all round. Unless you're hungry?"

"No, it's too late. Can you just cuddle me up?"

"It would be my pleasure."

Eight

I wake to an empty bed again, something that I'm not enjoying, and pull myself out of its warmth and comfort.

Seb is downstairs reading on his iPad at the kitchen table. Coffee steams from his mug.

"Morning, beautiful."

"Morning." I walk over and pour myself a small cup of coffee before joining Seb.

An uneasy silence builds in the air.

My head feels clogged with cotton wool and instead of looking forward to a day with Seb, I want to go and hide in our room.

"You look a little pale, Izzy. Are you feeling alright?"

"Yeah, just a little tired. Did you have any plans for today? It's the last weekend before Christmas."

"I need to check on some emails, and I also need to go and collect a few things in town. Nothing big." Our conversation is stifled, and I can't help think that the real world is making itself present in our relationship. It was bound to happen. Our whirlwind romance, the wedding and honeymoon. We needed to get back to normality at some point.

"Hey, what's up, Izzy? And remember that you are a rubbish liar."

"It isn't a big deal. I suppose I just miss the magic of the wedding and honeymoon. I just feel a little emotional. Maybe you can get what you need finished this morning, and we can have lunch together? Tomorrow is operation wrap the presents, and you're on sellotape duty."

"Sellotape duty?" Seb gives me a puzzled look.

"Yeah, I wrap, and you pass the tape."

Sunday is taken up with the mammoth wrapping task. Traditional brown paper and festive ribbons litter the floor of the front room. Boxes with pretty bows stack neatly under the tree with the presents piling up around it.

Seb has been a very efficient sellotape dispenser, and we've had fun. The disappointment from Friday night has faded. Next week we only have a few days before my parents arrive for their short visit. Christmas Eve to Boxing Day morning is plenty of time for us to catch up.

I stand up from my position on the floor and stretch out my back. A wave of nausea rises through me and has me holding my stomach.

"Izzy?"

"I'm fine. Just got up too fast."

"You've been off for days. Are you sure you're feeling okay? Maybe you should go to the doctor tomorrow?" I'd been tired, but until just now, I didn't think it was anything.

Panic rises, adding to the sickness as my mind rushes to an impossible conclusion. "I'm going to just… lie down for a while. I'm sure it's nothing." I rush upstairs and close the door as the tears storm to my eyes.

I can't be pregnant. I can't.

All of the plans we'd yet had the opportunity to make, the trips, the visits, the time spent together stream through my mind. None of that would be possible if we had a baby. I didn't want a baby. That had never crept into my mind, and we certainly hadn't discussed it.

I was being irrational. Apart from being tired and feeling a little sick, there were no other symptoms to have me thinking this. I suck back the tears and lie down on the bed. No. Seb and I have finally got our happy ever after. It wasn't going to be ruined now by something that neither of us wanted.

"I come with tea." Seb pokes his head around the door a few hours later. Luckily I'd dozed off, and I no longer felt sick or like bursting into tears.

"Thanks."

"You're welcome. Feeling better?"

"Much. I don't know what came over me."

"Are you going to see the doctor?"

"No, there's no need. I'm sure I'm just over doing it. Or I'm finally coming down from the adrenalin and excitement that's had me running at a hundred and ten percent the last few months."

"Okay. Look," Seb takes my hand, "we've only got a couple of days before Christmas and we won't have our own bubble like last year. Tuesday night I'd like to have you all to myself. I had very interesting plans for us at Solace, and I don't want to wait to share them." His sexy grin spreads across his face.

"Tuesday is my last day at work. I think we should celebrate."

"And I'll be working from home on Tuesday, so there will be no delays. I'll need to be in the office for a few hours on Wednesday morning, but I'll be home before your folks arrive."

"Perfect," I whisper the words while at the back of my mind the nagging doubt over my earlier panic remains.

* * *

Two days in the office is a long time when you're pre-occupied. Everywhere I looked I was reminded of the horrible thought that had slipped into my mind and taken root.

I was distracted and had to re-do the conversion statistics for one of my clients three times because I couldn't keep focused. I was in hell. Every time I considered the possibility of being pregnant, a sickening feeling hit. If Seb and I had a baby, our relationship would change irrevocably. We weren't ready to give up our time. At least I wasn't. I still wanted our time together to be just us.

The logical thing to do would be to buy a test and talk to Seb. But that will just make this all the more real. I was completely happy to live in 'fairy world' for the time being. I didn't want my sour mood to ruin the last evening we had on our own for a while either.

I put on my 'out of office' response and make my way home.

The lyrics to Winter Wonderland greet me as I push the front door open. The house is warm and scents of cinnamon and apple complete the Christmas feel. It dissolves my woes and traditional Christmas joy sparks inside of me.

"I'm in the kitchen, Izzy!"

I walk through and find Seb waiting with a candle lit table. Seb is pouring two glasses of wine and turns and offers me one.

"Cheers," he toasts.

"Cheers."

"To our first Christmas as husband and wife." We clink and I cast my eyes to the table.

"Are we eating?"

"Only something light. Italian Chicken. Take a seat."

Seb serves a small plate of chicken in a fragrant tomato and vegetable casserole. He joins me, and we dig in, the Christmas music filling the silence as we enjoy the juicy morsels.

My distraction of the last few days has dampened my sexual appetite, but I can tell from the look on Seb's face that he isn't suffering from the same. His eyes are always slightly hooded, and he's watching me like a hawk.

The delicious food is soon forgotten and the thrum of excitement kindles inside of me. I wait for Seb to speak, guiding the play of the evening.

"I want to keep the robe for when I take you to Solace. Make no mistake; you will be wearing it, and soon. Tonight, I want access to your body. Go upstairs and wait for me. Naked."

"Yes, Sir."

I quietly move from the kitchen, careful not to rush and enter the bedroom. Seb didn't tell me how long he'd be so I pull down the zip of my dress and wiggle out of it and slip the hold-ups off as I toe off my heels. I make short work of my bra and knickers and then pause. A flush rises over my skin as I wait expectantly.

My ears strain and I pick up the light thuds of his footfalls as he comes up the stairs. My heart skips to life, and I fidget in my place on the bed. All of the pent-up frustration from last week erupts within me.

Seb lingers in the doorway, making me wait longer. My gaze lowers, and I find a comfortable position to rest in. Knowing Seb, there is no set limit as to how long he'll leave me frustrated.

"I don't want to draw this out. We've both waited for this. I'm going to blindfold you, tie your hands and spank you, before making you come." My breath hitches as his words form pictures in my mind. My skin practically cries for his attention.

"I can see from your breathing that you like the thought of that. Stand up for me, baby." I slide off the bed and wait for him. I keep my gaze on the floor but want nothing more than to look up and get lost in his eyes.

He reads my body and tilts my head so that I can watch his pupils devour the aqua before he turns my world dark with the strip of silk. My body relaxes as I draw comfort from the familiar sensation.

"Hold your hands out to me." I present my hands and feel the soft glide of the silk around my wrists. I'm in Seb's hands now. A swarm of butterflies erupts in the pit of my stomach as my body anticipates his next move.

A bruising kiss lands on my lips. Seb holds me in place as he assaults me, stunning me into submission as he plunders my mouth.

"Umm. Now, lean over the edge of the bed, arms out in front. Legs spread wide so I can see your pussy." Seb's arm guides me around to the bed where I lean forward. A pillow cushions my chest, so I'm not at an awkward height. I inch my legs apart and rest my head to the side.

I take a few calming breaths.

I flinch at the first touch of Seb's hand. No matter how many times he does this, I can never fully anticipate his touch. He strokes my bum, patting it softly across one cheek and then the other. It soothes my racing heart as well as my skin.

Thwack! His palm smacks my skin, and the crack rings out around the room. My eyes close behind their silk cover, and I sink deeper into the bed. *Thwack! Thwack! Thwack!* Three more smacks in quick succession pull a gasp from me as the sting dissolves against my skin.

Seb finds his rhythm and intense heat burns across my backside. I sink into the feeling of being under his care and protection and relish the connection that my submission brings out in both of us.

He pauses, and I release a deep breath. He trails his finger through my pussy, and I groan in pleasure.

"Oh, baby. You're so wet. Do you want me to fuck you?"

"Yes, please, Sir."

"I don't think you're ready yet. Your skin isn't pink enough." His fingers dig into my bum as he pushes several fingers inside my waiting sex.

"Oh, god!" I mentally curse him but stay still. With my hands bound I can't grip on to the covers. I have to take everything he gives to me. *Thwack! Thwack!* "Yes!" My body tenses around his fingers with each strike. The flutter of my impending release ripples through me.

Thwack! Thwack!

Seb pumps his fingers after delivering his smacks, and I feel like I'm going to come apart from want. A stream of rambling murmurings plead with Seb as I get pulled further into the storm of my arousal. Need has overtaken my rational mind.

Seb's hot mouth covers my pussy before he dips his tongue into me. He anchors my legs apart, and I stretch onto my tip-toes as my muscles tense in the hope of orgasm.

His tongue fucks me and swirls over my clit sending a riot of sensation through me. He repeats his move and tips me over the edge.

"Yes... Seb... Yes!" I come loudly, pressing back against him as I ride out my climax. All energy floods from my body as I lay limp and exhausted on the bed.

"You taste delicious when you come, baby."

I don't even have the energy to smile at his sexy words.

A loud knock at the door re-focuses my hazy mind. Neither of us acknowledges it until it sounds again.

"Ignore it," I complain.

"Don't worry. I will," Seb purrs in my ear. His fingers release my wrists and the blindfold.

The knocking echoes through the house again, louder this time, and I can hear my phone ringing from downstairs. Clearly, someone wants our attention.

The look on Seb's face promises death. I pity whoever might be at the door. I hide my giggle as he moves to deal with the untimely interruption.

"Please don't go. We're not finished here."

"I'll be right back. They really aren't getting the message."

I watch Seb stalk out of the room and listen for the commotion that is sure to follow. Instead of the prompt slamming of the door all I hear is a few faint voices. The endorphins rushing around my blood soothe the annoyance I'd normally feel.

A few moments later, Seb appears at the bedroom door, looking decidedly put out.

"Your parents have decided to visit early," he grinds out.

"They're here?" I bolt upright in shock.

"Yes."

"Downstairs?"

"Yes, Izzy. I told them you were in the shower, so you better get your arse downstairs."

"Why did you let them in?"

"I couldn't turn them away, could I?"

I rush to the bathroom and grab my robe.

"Mum, I'll be down in a few minutes," I shout from the top of the stairs, mortified that they have turned up early and unannounced.

I turn back to Seb. "I'm so sorry." I gush at Seb.

"You know, next year we're going away. I want you to myself with no interruptions." Seb's usually the definition of control. I can see he's about to lose it.

Nine

"Mum, Dad, what are you doing here?" I ask as I enter the living room to greet them.

"We wanted to beat the holiday traffic tomorrow. We thought it would be a surprise."

"Well, it was certainly a surprise. Let me get you a cup of tea, and I'll go and get dressed. Seb will be down in a minute."

I make tea before heading back upstairs.

I can hear the shower running and slip into the bathroom. I open the door to see if I can try and relieve Seb but snatch my hand back as the icy water splashes on my arm.

"It's cold!"

"How else do you propose I calm myself down."

I lick my lips, feeling decidedly naughty and beckon Seb out of the shower.

"I warn you, Izzy. I'm not in a particularly pleased mood. If you get down on your knees, I'm going to fuck your mouth hard and fast."

I don't need to answer. Instead, I lower to my knees and wait for him to take what he needs. He turns the water off and steps from the shower.

He strokes his solid cock and holds it out for me. I wrap my lips around the tip and pull him deeper into my heat. His fingers tangle in my hair to hold me in place and prevent my withdrawal before he rolls his hips, pushing his shaft all the way to the back of my throat. I relax my jaw and let my tongue go to work, licking around the underside and the enflamed head as he pulls out before ramming back into my mouth.

He groans loudly as he drops his head back and finds a punishing pace that I struggle to keep up with. Saliva seeps from my mouth, aiding his strokes. He punches his way down my throat until I nearly gag as hot streams of come pour into my mouth.

"Fuck. I needed that. Thank you," Seb breaths out. I give him my best sexy smile.

"Come on. We need to look presentable for my parents."

"I might need to get back in the cold shower."

"Be my guest. I'll just admire the view."

Ten minutes later we both make it downstairs in a fit state to welcome my Mum and Dad. Seb makes tea while I give Mum a quick tour of the house.

"We're still renting until we find something that we fall in love with."

"This is quite some house, though, Izzy. Very nice."

I wait to see if she says anything further, but she doesn't.

The sudden urge to hear her question me about a family and children grates at my heart. I would never have wanted that in the past, hell, even last week. My thoughts are scattered all over the place.

We'd only moved here temporarily. I didn't want Seb to buy a house simply because he could. Perhaps now was the right time to reconvene our search?

"Izzy?" Mum looks at me expectantly.

"Sorry, yes?"

"Are we done?"

"Oh, yes. I'll get Seb to bring up your bags." I lead Mum back into the kitchen where, by the sounds of things, Seb and my father are talking sports.

"So, now that we're here do you have any plans for tomorrow?" Mum looks expectantly at me.

"Not really, sorry Mum. I was going to give the house a once-over before you arrived. Seb has to work in the morning."

"That's fine. We can certainly look after ourselves. Perhaps we could pop into Bath for some last minute shopping?"

"Really, Diane? On Christmas Eve?" Dad detests shopping at the best of times, let alone on one of the busiest shopping days of the year. I catch the frosty glare she throws his way and hide my smirk with my cup of tea.

"Perhaps we can discuss it at breakfast. If you don't mind, I'm going to get an early night. I want to make the most of tomorrow now that we're here."

"I'll bring your bags up, Diane." Seb leaves the kitchen with Mum.

"It's good to see you happy again, kiddo." Dad puts his arm around me and pulls me to his side. He's not the most affectionate, but these small gestures, when they do come, mean the world.

"Thanks, Dad. I am."

"Sorry about the early arrival. Your mother can be… insistent."

"It's fine. Although a little warning would have been nice."

"Right. I better be going to bed as well. Seems like there will be shopping on the agenda tomorrow. Night, kiddo."

"Night, Dad."

"I can't believe our luck. I'm sorry about this evening." I pull back the duvet and climb into bed.

"I'm trying to see the funny side. I suppose it's not every day you're interrupted in the middle of sex."

"By your in-laws." Laughter erupts from my chest, and I slam a hand over my mouth before rolling into Seb's warm body. He pulls me against him and holds me tight.

My giggling ceases when my mind skips forward nine months and the thought of a baby in our lives. We'd constantly be interrupted. We'd have another person to put first and prioritise over anything that we wanted. This is our first Christmas as husband and wife, and we've not even managed to celebrate together. There won't be any other opportunities if I'm pregnant.

"Are you going to go shopping with your Mum tomorrow?"

"Maybe."

"Hey, what's wrong?"

"I just wish we'd been able to have some time for us. It seems that whenever we try, life gets in the way."

"There's going to be plenty of time for us. We might have been on a clock in the past, but that's not how things are now, and they haven't been for a while. What's brought all of this on?"

"Christmas, maybe. Getting back to a normal life?"

"But that's what I want with you. I've waited a long time for this. For you. I love you, and I love our life together. The D/s as well as the normal day-to-day and mundane."

"And I love you." I look up to see worry etched on Seb's handsome face.

"You need to tell me what's got you so out of sorts."

"What do you want in the future? We're still in this house. We haven't talked about family or anything like that. I suppose I've got some questions that's all." I brace for the conversation I never wanted to initiate, but can't help but need to know.

"I wanted to have you in our own home a long time ago. Renting was a compromise. I learnt that I couldn't push you too hard or too fast. It worked because you're now my wife." He places a loving kiss on the top of my head as I snuggle in closer to his body. "We can look for a house in the new year. I know you wanted to contribute, and you have the money to do it. Maybe now's the right time. As for a family, I've never given it much consideration."

"Okay. That sounds like a plan."

I lie in silence, calmed by the steady rise and fall of Seb's chest.

"Good night," I whisper.

"Night, baby."

My eyes may have closed, but sleep evades me. A hundred things are racing through my mind. I know I was vague about what was on my mind, and Seb will no doubt be disappointed that I didn't tell him the full truth about what worried me. Some couples would give anything to be parents. Shouldn't I be excited about this possibility?

I'm restless for what feels like the rest of the night. However, I'm asleep when Seb wakes me in the morning to say goodbye.

"I'll be back by one, I promise."

"See you later. Love you."

"I love you."

I think I made the decision before I drifted to sleep last night. I need to find out if I am pregnant or not. I can't keep wondering and make plans or decisions that may never be warranted.

The electronic bell surprises me as I push open the door to the local pharmacy. Christmas displays greet me as I take a quick look around to find the family planning section. I take in the assortment of choices that exist to find out if I'm pregnant. Early response, digital test, single or double, ovulation kits. I grab what looks like a fail-safe test and take it to the till.

"That certainly will be a special Christmas present," the older lady comments as she rings up the sale.

"Pardon?"

"Your test. I hope it goes the way you want."

I hand her the money with what I'm sure is a grimace covering my face.

"Merry Christmas."

"Yes, Merry Christmas." I stuff the test back in my bag and rush out of the store.

Mum and Dad have braved the Christmas shoppers, so I have the house to myself when I arrive home. I head to the kitchen and pour a large glass of water before downing it all at once.

A sick ball of nerves poisons my stomach and turns me into a juddering wreck. Christmas was meant to be my happy time, not something I dreaded. God, how was I going to tell Seb if I *was* pregnant? Would he resent me for burdening him with a baby so soon after marrying me?

I snatch up the test and go upstairs to the bedroom. My fingers dig through the cardboard packaging for the white and blue test. I follow the instructions and then set the timer on my phone for three minutes and wait.

It is amazing how long three minutes can be when the result will change your life forever. I pace the bedroom unable to keep still. My heart stampedes in my chest as the nerves get the better of me.

After an age, the alarm sounds in the bathroom, ringing pleasantly as if it has good news. I grab the plastic stick and turn it over, my eyes honing in on the little box with the result.

The blue line runs horizontally through the window. No plus sign. Not pregnant.

A sob bursts from my chest and echoes in the bathroom. I drop the test and seal my mouth with my hand to stop any more outbursts, but it is all in vain. Tears stream from my eyes as I collapse onto our bed. I weep hard, body-wrenching tears.

I should be happy. I didn't want to be pregnant. I didn't want my life with Seb to change so soon.

"Izzy? Are you home?" I hear Mum call from the hall. I can't control my cries enough to answer her and just continue to blub.

"Izzy? Darling, what's wrong?" Mum's at the door to our room and takes one look at me before opening her arms to me.

"Shh shh shh. What's the matter? I'm sure it can be fixed."

"I'm… not… pregnant," I stutter out.

"Oh, dear. You don't need to start worrying yet. I'm sure you can't have been trying for long." She strokes down my back trying to soothe my hysterics.

"No. I didn't... want to be pregnant."

"And now you're sad?"

"Yes! How can I be upset... over something I didn't want?" I sniff as more tears trail down my face. Mum gently sways us as we sit on the edge of the bed, our arms wrapped around one another.

I cling to my mum as I've never done in the past. Confusion plagues my mind as my emotions cascade through me.

"Have you talked to Seb?"

"No. He doesn't even know I took a test."

"Why would you keep this from him?"

"Because I don't know how he feels about children. I didn't want kids. I didn't want to be pregnant. What was the point of telling him until I knew?"

"And now you don't know what to do or how you feel?"

"Yes." Another wave of sobs tumble from me at my confession. I don't know how I feel about any of this.

"Tuck yourself up into bed. I'll go and bring you a cup of tea and send Seb up when he gets back. You need to talk to him about all of this."

"Thanks, Mum." I gingerly unlock my hold of her and crawl into bed. She gently smoothes the hair from my face as my eyes close in emotional exhaustion. I focus on her touch and will my mind to shut off until I can talk through all of this with Seb.

I don't notice when she leaves, but I do notice when Seb takes her place.

"Iz, your Mum said you needed to talk to me." I peel my eyes open and see Seb lying on his side next to me. His eyes are more blue than green in this light, and I wonder if our children would have my eyes or his?

My throat feels itchy and dry, and my eyes are sore from the tears, but I feel calmer than I did earlier.

"What's the time?" I ask.

"Just past one. Want to tell me what's going on? And I'd appreciate the full story now." I don't miss the undercurrent of annoyance from Seb. I can't blame him.

I pull myself up and throw myself around Seb, squeezing him so there're only the layers of our clothes between us.

"I thought I was pregnant," I mumble against his neck.

"Okay. And?"

"I'm not." Tears creep back into my eyes and burn my throat as I struggle to keep the emotion inside.

"Did you want us to be?"

"No. But then I took the test, and it was negative, and I was sad."

"So you *did* want us to be."

"I'm not sure. All I know is that I'm feeling teary and mixed up right now, and we've not even talked about kids, and I've landed all of this on you."

"Baby," Seb pulls my face from hiding, and he tilts my head up with gentle thumbs, so I'm looking into his eyes. "No, we've not discussed children. Would I have a baby with you? Absolutely. Would I be happy if you were pregnant now? Yes. Am I happy that you've kept this from me and skirted around the truth for the last week or so? No. I'm already looking forward to your punishment."

"I didn't even know how I felt about all of this. I didn't know what to say." My defence is feeble.

"We communicate with each other. That's always been our rule, and when we stop following it, things get messed up. Now, want to tell me why you're so upset?"

Safely wrapped in Seb's arms, and with the initial shock and questions out the way, I relax and open up about my worries and fears. I don't leave anything out and confess how selfish I felt about having to share our time with a baby.

"I don't think it's selfish that you want time for us. I want that too. And lately, it's been more difficult than it has been in the past. Life can get in the way sometimes, but we always need to make time for each other. We can work on that."

"So, you wouldn't mind if we had a baby and turned our worlds upside down?"

"I'd say that I'd rather plan for a baby and agree when we both thought the time was right for us, rather than have a surprise pregnancy. Although there is something amazingly sexy about the thought of you pregnant with my child." Seb's stubble grazes my cheek as he kisses my throat and neck, moving towards my lips to kiss me.

"Do you want to have a baby, Izzy?"

"Not in nine months, but yes. I think I do." I smile. A sense of relief warms my heart. Seb's answering smile has my heart bursting with love.

"Okay then. Do you feel better now that we've talked?"

"Yes. Part of me knew I should have mentioned something. But I was so unsure of how I felt. I didn't want to say anything until I knew for sure. I didn't expect to be this upset." I can't help but feel foolish for all the drama I've caused. Seb just keeps me cuddled to him.

"I know it's only Christmas Eve, but perhaps we could start our own tradition." Seb releases me and rolls to his side of the bed and opens the top drawer. He hands me an envelope wrapped in a red satin ribbon.

"What's this?" I sit up and wipe the remaining tears from my face.

"Your Christmas gift."

"Are we doing gifts on Christmas Eve now, because I think I'd love you even more than I already do if we can." My excitement bubbles over as I look between Seb and the envelope that's burning a hole in my hands.

"Yes, we can." At his words, I prise the thick envelope open and pull out a glossy card with a photo of an impressive sail-shaped hotel perched on the edge of a beach. I pull the remaining folded sheets of paper from the envelope and scan the words.

Confirmation… hotel stay… Barcelona… April…

"We're going to Barcelona?"

"Yes. I thought a short break would be just what we'd want."

"We've only just come back from New York?"

"And?"

"I don't know. I suppose," my words fade on my lips. "Thank you. It looks amazing, and I can't wait. Thank you." I had to start accepting that Seb treated me like a princess at times and there didn't need to be an ulterior motive.

"You're welcome. I meant what I said last night. We can start looking for our home. I haven't pushed for it, but I want us settled. We can keep in mind space for children." My eyes burn with more unshed tears. I still had to pinch myself at how different my life was now.

"Oh, your gift. It's under the tree." I pull away from Seb wanting to reciprocate in our new Christmas Eve tradition.

"No you don't." He pulls me back to him. "We can get it later. I want to make sure we're good before I release you back to your parents."

"Oh, God, they're still here."

"Yes, sweetheart," he chortles. "They're fine, though. They were having lunch when I came up."

"You're wonderful, you know that?"

"No, but you can keep telling me that."

"You always know what I need even if I don't."

"That's part of being your Husband and your Dom. It's my job to anticipate your needs. I want you happy, Izzy. Always. We've come so far in the last few months. I don't want any doubt or worry between us."

"I'm sorry."

"Shh, don't be sorry. I don't want tears. This is our first Christmas together, and although we might have company, we have a few days before the New Year to ourselves. Next year we can plan for a white Christmas in New York. What do you think?"

"I'd like that, Sir."

"Happy Christmas, Izzy."

"Happy Christmas. Seb."

The End

Surrender to More

Trust. *A simple notion for some, but impossibly out of reach for Jessica Riley.*

The walls around her heart are built high from betrayal and years of keeping everyone at arm's length. She's happy with the way her life is, or so she thought.

Hard core Dom, Lucas Clark, was immediately drawn to Jessica. As their paths continue to cross, Lucas tests Jessica's submissive nature, as well as her steadfast resolve to keep her emotions out of her relationships. He wants more than just sex. He demands Jess' trust. The one thing she keeps locked away.

As their bond intensifies, Jessica fears that this Greek God will put the pieces of her heart back together. Family, marriages and ghosts of her past all plague her ability to trust her own decisions, especially the ones that revolve around love.

A woman who's afraid of heart break fights her own surrender against the man who doesn't let her play it safe anymore.

Other Books by Rachel De Lune

More

An unexpected encounter in a bar promises Isabel Fields a chance to change her life. Sexual dominant Sebastian York, leads her on a passionate journey of sexual awakening that satisfies everything she's craved.

Their casual arrangement soon grows too confining as Sebastian ignites Isabel's long-buried desires and touches her heart. However, Sebastian may not prove to be the love of Izzy's life and just might leave her wanting more…

Other Books by Rachel De Lune

Forever More

What if you had everything you wanted within your grasp, but let it go?

Isabel Fields stands on the brink of a new life. She has the Dominant/submissive relationship she craves with the man she loves, but her past continues to haunt her.

With Isabel, Sebastian York can release the sexual Alpha Male he'd always tempered. He doesn't intend to let her go, even when she bolts in panic. Together, both could experience the freedom to explore their relationship and sides of themselves previously stifled.

Their love is tested when issues of trust rising from Izzy's past marriage and her damaged heart take their toll. They may have fallen in love, but that doesn't guarantee it will be forever more.

Izzy and Seb have two choices: grow stronger together or be pulled apart by the past.

About Rachel De Lune

Rachel De Lune writes emotionally driven erotic romance. She began scribbling her stories in the pages of a notebook several years ago. Today, she's still scribbling stories of dominance and submission.

Rachel lives in the South West of England & daydreams about shoes, lingerie and chocolate, in-between being a mum and a wife.

For every woman who's ever desired more. www.racheldelune.com

Connect with Rachel De Lune:

Facebook:
http://on.fb.me/1FXxBwa
Twitter:
https://twitter.com/rachel_de_lune
Google+:
https://plus.google.com/103010030570874602054/posts
Goodreads:
https://www.goodreads.com/user/show/19186002-rachel-de-lune
Pinterest:
http://www.pinterest.com/RachelDelune/
AUTHOR WEBSITE:
http://www.racheldelune.com/

Thank you for reading *A Little Something More*.

We often update our books when grammar errors are found, so please let us know if you've found one at:
stephanie@trollriverpub.com

Other Great Books from Troll River Publications

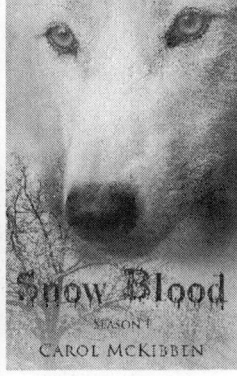

KINGS OF GUARDIAN
BOOK 1
KRIS MICHAELS

Lovely
ELITE DOMS of WASHINGTON BOOK 1
ELIZABETH SaFLEUR

For every woman who's ever desired ...
More
The Evermore Series
Rachel De Lune

In the currents of the heart,
beware of love. It's an
Underlow
Kris Michaels
Rachel De Lune
Elizabeth Sa Fleur
Patricia A. Knight

Made in the USA
Columbia, SC
13 February 2018